Guard Goose!

'Guard Goose!'
An original concept by Elizabeth Dale
© Elizabeth Dale

Illustrated by Giusi Capizzi

Published by MAVERICK ARTS PUBLISHING LTD
Studio 3A, City Business Centre, 6 Brighton Road,
Horsham, West Sussex, RH13 5BB
© Maverick Arts Publishing Limited May 2019
+44 (0)1403 256941

A CIP catalogue record for this book is available at the British Library.

ISBN 978-1-84886-445-0

www.maverickbooks.co.uk

This book is rated as: Turquoise Band (Guided Reading)

Guard Goose!

by **Elizabeth Dale**
illustrated by **Giusi Capizzi**

It was dark. Every animal on the farm was fast asleep – except for Gertie the goose.

Gertie wanted to be useful, like the other animals. 'This is my big chance!' she thought. 'Go, Gertie, go!'

Gertie flew up onto the farmhouse roof. She opened her big beak...

HONK! HONK! HONK!

All the farm animals woke up – including Ronnie the rooster. "What are you doing, Gertie?" they called.

"I'm doing Ronnie's job for him. I'm

waking you up!" Gertie honked happily.

"But it's only midnight!" they all cried.

"We don't get up for hours." 7

It was difficult to get back to sleep and the next day everyone was tired. Bess the sheepdog lay snoozing in the sun.

Farmer Daisy whistled for her to come and round up the sheep - but Bess didn't hear. But Gertie did.

"This is my big chance to be useful!"

she said. She flew to the sheep field.

"Go, Gertie, go! Hiss! Hiss! Snap!"

9

She tried rounding up the sheep. But the sheep were terrified! They all ran away.

"What are you doing, Gertie?" Ronnie clucked.

"I'm doing Bess's job for her. I'm rounding up the sheep!" Gertie honked happily.

"But you aren't rounding them up!" clucked Ronnie. "Look! You're sending them everywhere!"

Whoops!

Gertie was sad. She'd really wanted to help. But she'd made things worse. It took Farmer Daisy and Bess a long time to find all the sheep.

When Farmer Daisy finished, she was very
tired. She flopped down into her big old
armchair. "I'm hungry, but I'm too tired to
cook dinner," she sighed.

'This is my big chance to be useful,' Gertie thought. 'Go, Gertie, go!' And she started cooking Farmer Daisy's dinner.

Soon, Gertie spilled the milk...

...dropped the flour...

...and smashed a plate.

The noise woke Farmer Daisy.

"Oh, Gertie, what a mess!" she cried.

"I'll have to clean this up, before I start

making my dinner!"

Then she slipped over in the spilt milk.

"Let me help!" said Gertie.

But on her way to help, Gertie knocked over a bottle...

....which knocked over the tea pot...

....which knocked over the mug.

Tea went everywhere.

"Go, Gertie, go!" cried Farmer Daisy.

"I've had enough of you trying to be

useful. Go away!"

Gertie was so sad. She loved the farm and all the animals on it.

But Farmer Daisy was right. If she couldn't be useful, then she should go away.

But the animals all loved her and were sad to see her leave. "Don't go, Gertie!" cried the cows and donkeys.

Only the sheep didn't say anything. They were too busy running around and baaing like crazy. Two men were rounding them up, waving sticks.

Gertie was cross. The men were upsetting the sheep. Honking loudly, Gertie chased after them and pecked their ankles hard!

"Go, Gertie, Go!" baaed all the sheep.

"OUCH! OUCH!" cried the men. They ran away, and Gertie chased them all the way back to their truck.

Farmer Daisy heard the noise and came running down the drive. 'Whoops!' thought Gertie. Now she was in even more trouble!

"Well done, Gertie!" cried Farmer Daisy. "You've saved all the sheep from the sheep-thieves!"

Gertie hadn't known the men were

sheep-thieves!

"I'm sorry I told you to go," said Farmer

Daisy, "I was tired and I didn't mean it.

I love you, my silly goose."

Gertie's heart lifted.

"Will you be our Guard Goose?

You'd be brilliant at it!" Farmer

Daisy said.

Gertie honked happily.

She could stay! And she finally

had a job of her own.

So, from that day on, Gertie kept all the

animals safe by chasing strangers off the farm.

She loved doing it. And she was useful at last!

"Gertie, you're the best Guard Goose!"

all the animals cried.

Unfortunately, the new postman

didn't agree!

Quiz

1. Who is awake at the beginning of the story?
a) The sheep
b) Ronnie the rooster
c) Gertie the goose

2. What does Gertie want to be?
a) Useful
b) Loud
c) Funny

3. Gertie spilled the milk... dropped the flour... and smashed a _____.
a) Armchair
b) Cup
c) Plate

4. How does Gertie save the sheep from the sheep-thieves?
a) She honks at the postman
b) She pecks their ankles
c) She tells Farmer Daisy

5. Who isn't happy about Gertie's new job in the end?
a) The postman
b) The cows
c) Bess the sheepdog

Turn over for answers

Book Bands for Guided Reading

The Institute of Education book banding system is a scale of colours that reflects the various levels of reading difficulty. The bands are assigned by taking into account the content, the language style, the layout and phonics. Word, phrase and sentence level work is also taken into consideration.

Maverick Early Readers are a bright, attractive range of books covering the pink to white bands. All of these books have been book banded for guided reading to the industry standard and edited by a leading educational consultant.

To view the whole Maverick Readers scheme, visit our website at

www.maverickearlyreaders.com

Or scan the QR code above to view our scheme instantly!

Quiz Answers: 1c, 2a, 3c, 4b, 5a